Published by
Five Acre Publishing
Gresham, Oregon

Copyright by Allan Zion 2018

Book jacket designed by Grandpa Owl
Illustrations by Grandpa Owl, Brynley and Lainey

ISBN 978-1-5323-7649-8

About the Author

Allan Zion lives in Gresham, Oregon with his wife Patti. He is a retired engineer, salesman and musician. The ideas for his Farley adventures come from his 8 year old twin granddaughters, Brynley and Lainey who live with their parents in a home with a five acre field.

Acknowledgements

Thanks to all my family and friends for their encouragement to put these stories on paper. And to my editor, Alex Wienbrecht and author friend Alice Cotton, a very heartfelt "Thank You!"

A very special thanks to my readers/consultants and illustrators Brynley and Lainey

The Adventures of

Farley
The Field Mouse

Book 1

Lost!

Written by **Allan Zion**

Consultants Brynley and Lainey

A Five Acre Field Adventure

Table of Contents

Chapter 1

Farley the field mouse was a

friendly little mouse, sort of round

and always happy. If you asked

Farley he would tell you that he lived

in the biggest field in the world, but

being so small, could only imagine

how big it was. He had never been
any farther away from his burrow
than the nearest blade of grass, which
really wasn't very far at all. His
burrow was in a little hollow in the
middle of a five acre field. The
meadow grass was tall and ripe with
seeds, providing plenty of shade,
except in the fall when the mower
would cut down the grass for hay.
Even then there was enough left for a
good place to live, cool in the summer
and warm in the winter.

Once, when he felt
adventurous, he climbed on a mound
of rocks near his burrow and saw tall
fir trees at the edge of the meadow.
He knew the trees were a place for the
birds to nest and raise their families.

He also knew that Edgar the Eagle stayed in one of those trees when he hunted above the five acre field. Farley was always afraid of seeing Edgar because it meant that the eagle was hunting for his next meal. While standing on the mound he also saw a large shiny spot that sparkled when the wind blew. He learned later it was pool of water called a lake.

But most days Farley had no reason to go any farther than the seeds that fell off the grass, because that was his breakfast, lunch and dinner, with

occasional nuts and berries for

dessert.

Chapter 2

Today Farley, dressed in his blue
vest, was feeling a little lonely
because none of his friends had come
by to see him. His friends were other
animals that lived around the field.
So, having eaten his lunch of seeds
and nuts, Farley set off across the
field to see if he could find somebody
to talk with.

It was a warm day and as he walked
he daydreamed a little and didn't pay
attention to what was happening

around him. He didn't notice the

shadow on the ground until he was

quite far away from his burrow.

When he looked up he saw Edgar the

Eagle and ran toward a fallen log.

Farley was certain he was going to be

Edgar's noon meal and ran faster. He

got to the log and was able to crawl

under it to hide.

Even with his keen eyesight Edgar couldn't see Farley so he flew away, hunting for something else to eat. Farley took a deep breath and peeked out, getting ready to run again.

"That was pretty close," he heard behind him. It was Betsy, a small brown rabbit and a friend that lived in the field with her family. She had on her vegetable hunting overalls and Farley guessed she was looking for something to eat. "Edgar was heading for me when he saw you and I guess he decided you'd make a better meal. I just made it under this log. Thank you for saving me!"

"You're welcome," Farley said,

"I'm glad I could help. I'm glad that Edgar didn't get me."

Farley peeked out from under the log.
"I wonder where we are," he said.
"I've never been this far away from
my home before."

"I don't know but I'm sure we can
find out." Betsy said.

Betsy hopped up on the log and over
the grass.

"Follow me, Farley." she yelled.

Farley, with his tiny legs, couldn't
hop like Betsy. He yelled for Betsy to
slow down but before long he

couldn't see her and discovered that

he was lost!

Chapter 3

"What do I do now? " Farley thought to himself. He had never been lost before. He was scared and felt very alone. Nothing looked familiar and he had no idea which way to go. He sat on a clump of weeds. He was sitting there thinking about what to do when he heard sounds coming from the field directly in front of him. Farley crawled under the thick underbrush, getting his vest dirty and his chin tickled at the same time.

At the edge of the brush he came to a

small flat spot in the field. When he

looked out through the grass he saw a

large gray bird with yellow feet and a

yellow beak. Farley had never seen a

bird like this before. It looked a little

like his friend Donny the duck but much bigger and had a long neck.

"Oh dear, I hope this isn't another thing wanting to eat me!" Farley thought.

The big bird looked down at Farley and said "Honk, honk what are you doing down there in the grass you silly field mouse? Don't you know that Edgar is hunting today? He'll probably see you there. Come under my shadow so I can hide you." the strange bird said to Farley.

Farley took a deep breath and ran to the bird and stepped into it's shadow on the ground.

"Are you a duck?" Farley asked.

"Don't be silly. I am a goose and we are so much more grand than ducks. My name is Gertrude and I live at the farm over the hill. Imagine calling me a duck. I am certainly not one of those! Who are you?"

Before Farley could answer they were interrupted by a voice coming from behind him. The new voice belonged to Donny the duck and he was walking out of the brush toward Farley and the big bird. Donny was an old pal and Farley was happy to see him.

"Don't mind her, Farley. Gertrude thinks she is the boss of the barnyard because she is so big, but mostly she just talks a lot. I saw Edgar flying and thought he might be after some food," Donny said, "So I started looking to see who might be on the menu. When I saw Gertrude I decided to stay here. She's so big that Edgar wouldn't bother with her. What are you doing way over here?"

"I had to hide from Edgar. I found Betsy the rabbit but she hopped too fast for me to keep up. I didn't see anything familiar and realized that I was lost. I heard Gertrude honking while I was hiding in the brush. She saw me at the edge of the grass and hid me under her body. That's when you came along. Can either of you show me the way to my home?"

Farley asked.

"Well, I have never been there,"

Gertrude said. "Donny, can you take

Farley home?"

"I haven't been to his house, either,"

Donny said. "Don't have any idea

how to get there."

"We must find someone to take

Farley home, Gertrude said. "Let's

go up to the barn and see who's

around today. Come along, Farley.

You'll have to run fast to keep up

with me. I don't want Edgar to see

you so stay under my body."

Chapter 4

The little group started walking
toward the building on the other side
of the water that Donny called a lake.
Gertrude led the little parade with a
waddling, swaying gait. Donny
followed with his bobbing, bouncy
steps and Farley ran fast, trying to
keep up.

"Be careful around the lake. Other
animals live there that might not be as
nice as me and Gertrude." Donny
whispered to Farley.

Just as they were walking out of the

grass at the edge of the water they

saw a strange looking furry animal.

He looked like he was wearing a mask

and had a long bushy tail with rings

on it.

He was staring into the water. Farley

pushed closer to the big goose. He was getting scared again.

"That's Ricky the raccoon" Gertrude said, "He won't bother us, he's probably looking for frogs or fish for his dinner."

Just then something in the water started to splash loudly and Ricky jumped up and ran into the tall bushes. Out of the water came a huge animal with a long snout, full of teeth and a body all covered with what looked like squares of leather.

26

"Look out!" Donny yelled, "It's Albert the alligator. Quick, run back to the tall grass."

Back they ran into the brush and hid until the monster walked back toward the water.

"Albert lives around the lake and will eat anything." Donny whispered. Donny took a quick look and saw that Albert was crawling back into the lake.

"I think we better take the high road to the barn. Grab my leg and hang on, and keep an eye out for Edgar."

Gertrude said.

Chapter 5

Farley climbed up on Gertrude's foot

and wrapped his arms around the leg.

Gertrude and Donny

both flew up in the air and across the

lake. Farley held tight to Gertrude's

leg and shivered with fright. He had

never done anything so exciting

before. He held on for dear life and

shouted.

"Look at me, I'm flying just like a

bird. I can see forever."

The lake didn't look as big from the

air as it did from the ground, Farley

thought to himself as they landed

quickly on the far side. Farley

stepped off Gertrudes foot and gave a

little sigh of relief. Over his shoulder

he heard a sharp yapping bark.

"Donny, I think I hear a dog. I had better hide!" Farley said.

"Don't be afraid, Farley, it's my friend Rowdy the red fox. We have been pals for a long time. He won't eat me because my feathers would get stuck in his mouth" Donny quacked.

Rowdy was walking toward them from the direction of a small shed and Farley thought he sure looked like a dog. As he got closer he saw that the fox was not as big as the dogs he had seen in the field. He had beautiful red fur with white on his chest and a big bushy tail with a white tip. His big white teeth made Farley nervous and he started looking for a place to hide.

"Don't worry, Farley. Rowdy won't try to eat you." Donny said.

"I won't bother with you, little mouse because you are too small," the red fox said, "Besides, any friend of Donny's is a friend of mine."

"Let's stop all the gabbin' and get to the barn!" Gertrude honked.

Chapter 6

Off they went through the grass. Once again it was Gertrude leading the way with Donny, Farley and Rowdy following along as best they could. Before long they came to a big red building with wide doors and hay hanging out of a window high above the ground.

"Let's see who we can talk to," said Donny. "Maybe someone will know the way to Farley's home."

They all walked into the building through the big doors.

"It's kind of dark in here." Farley said, as he crawled under some dry hay.

He looked around the room. Bales of hay and buckets were lying on the ground and ropes and other things were hanging from pegs on the wall. Above him was another floor that looked like it had things stored on it.

Farley heard a munching sound and discovered he was about to go into something's mouth! Something with very big teeth!

"Help." Farley yelled.

"Don't squeak so loud, or I might get scared and step on you!"

The voice came from very high above Farley's head. He looked up and saw a huge, long face with large brown eyes staring down at him.

"Hello, little fella. I'm Hortense. I'm a farm horse and used to pull a plow for the farmer and dig up the field for planting. Farmer Henderson got a big tractor so I don't have to work hard anymore. Now I just take care of the barn. Who are you and what are you doing here?'

"My name is Farley and I'm a field mouse and I'm lost. All I want to do is go home," Farley replied. "Do you know where I live?"

Hortense looked down at the little mouse.

"First you better move out of my hay pile so I can finish my lunch. This is not a very good place to carry on a conversation."

"Sorry," Farley said and he jumped out of the hay, "I didn't know it was your lunch."

"Quite all right, quite all right,"
Hortense said, "No harm done. Now,
where is this place where you live?"

"I wish I knew," Farley said, "It's
out in the field somewhere. I got
chased by Edgar the eagle and lost my
way."

"I really don't have any idea where it
might be," Hortense said, "Let's go
up to the farmer's house, and ask
there. Hop up on that bale of hay and
grab my tail. It's pretty thick so you
can climb up and get onto my back.

You can ride up there so you won't get stepped on. Let me know when you're ready."

Farley jumped up on the bale and climbed up Hortense's tail and onto her back.

"I'm ready." Farley said.

Chapter 7

All the animals started toward the farmhouse. It was getting to be quite a parade with all the animals walking along in a line. They soon came to a small, white house with an open window on the side.

As Farley looked into the open window he heard another strange sound.

"Awk, awk, who's out there?" said a raspy voice coming from the other side of the window.

Farley had no idea what kind of

animal had a voice like that.

"It's me. Hortense," the horse said.

"I'm with Donny and Gertrude. This

is Farley on my back. He's a little

field mouse I just met. Is that

you Pete?

 "Awk, sure is. Who else would be

sitting in my cage?" Pete the Parakeet

said. He was a small pretty bird, about

the size of Farley, with yellow and

green feathers and big eyes. He was

sitting on a little swing in a large cage. The cage hung from a stand that sat on the floor by the window. The little bird had a good view of the field.

"Farley, the field mouse has lost his way and we are looking for someone who might know how he can get home." Hortense said.

"Well," Pete said, looking out the window at Hortense and Farley, "I would like to help you but I'm in here all the time and can only see the field

from this window. Why don't we ask

Polly the kitten?'

"She plays in the field everyday and

might have seen Farleys' burrow. She

should be around the house

somewhere."

"Awk, Awk,. Polly please come to my cage. Big problem here." Pete yelled.

Chapter 8

"Meow, did I hear my name?"

A little yellow tabby cat walked into

the room. "Who's got big problems?"

the tabby asked.

"Farley the field mouse does," Pete

said "He's lost and can't find his way

home. Can you help find it for him?"

" I don't know exactly where he

lives but I'm sure I could get him very

close. Polly answered. "I remember

seeing him eating seeds out there in

the field one day. We better not try to

look now because I see Edgar up in the sky looking for something to catch and I don't want to be it."

"Maybe I can help," said a familiar voice from under the window.

Polly jumped up onto the window sill. She, Farley and Hortense looked down to see Rowdy looking up at them.

"I came over to see what was going on and heard Polly talking about Edgar. Edgar chases me every day. I don't know why he keeps doin' it, because he can never catch me. I will run across the yard and lead him away from here so you can go into the field and find Farley's home."

"Oh thank you, Rowdy. I don't know what to say." Farley said.

"Just say goodbye and I will lead Edgar away. Don't dilly-dally here when I'm gone. Just go!" Rowdy yelled, running out into the yard.

Sure enough, Edgar saw Rowdy and flew straight toward him. Rowdy ran behind the barn, under a shed, through a fence and out into the woods. Edgar

flew as fast as he could trying to catch

Rowdy, but Rowdy was too quick,

ducking in and out of the trees and

bushes as he led Edgar away from the

farm house.

Chapter 9

"Quick, climb up my mane and up
onto my head between my ears."
Hortense said to Farley. "Polly, you
climb up too, and we'll go into the
field and see if we can find Farley's
home."

Farley did what Hortense said and Polly jumped from the window sill and onto the horses back. Off they went in to the field. Gertrude, Donny and Pete waved goodbye.

Hortense walked slowly so Farley and Polly wouldn't fall off. They walked awhile until Polly yelled and pointed to a clump of bushes and grass stalks.

"I think I see something familiar," she said. "Yes, it's the blueberry bush where I've seen Farley eating his breakfast. Walk over that way."

"I was there yesterday," Farley cried "It's near where I live."

"Careful, Hortense, don't step in that hole." Polly yelled.

Hortense almost put her foot into Farley's home.

"That's my burrow!" cried Farley, "I'm home!"

Farley and Polly ran across Hortense's back and down her tail and jumped to the ground where they danced around, happy to have found the little burrow

"You must stay and have sweet mint tea and seed cakes with me." Farley said to Hortense and Polly.

Farley hurried into his kitchen to fix the food for his guests.

Of course the burrow was too small for Hortense and Polly so they had their picnic on the grass in the front yard and enjoyed the end of the day. The seed cakes were delicious and the tea was warm and sweet. Hortense ate some grass to go with the small,

field mouse sized seed cakes.

In time they finished eating and

relaxed. They were all content with

the meal and the warm sunshine.

After a while Hortense and Polly said

it was time for them to go and saying

goodbye, headed for home.

Chapter 10

The sun was dipping into the west, and Farley sat quietly, thinking about all that had happened that day and the adventures that he'd had with his new friends, Gertrude, Ricky, Rowdy, Hortense, Pete and Polly. And of course his old friends Donny and Betsy.

"What great friends they are, all except Edgar. He is kind of a pain," he thought. "And I don't mind not meeting Albert the alligator. What a

day. I should write all this down so I

won't forget."

As if he could ever forget!

Farley got a pad of paper and a pencil

from the storage box on the shelf

above his dresser. He sat down at his kitchen table and began writing about his adventure in the five acre field.

The moon began to rise and Farley wondered what tomorrow would bring.

Will he have more adventures, meet new friends?

We'll see.